THE OFFICIAL
NEWCASTLE UNITED FC
ANNUAL 2015

Written by Mark Hannen
Designed by Lucy Boyd

Thanks to Tom Easterby, Michael Bolam, Ben Ashley, Amanda Brennan, Andrew Simpson and Paul Joannou.

A Grange Publication

© 2014. Published by Grange Communications Ltd., Edinburgh, under licence from Newcastle United Football Club. Printed in the EU.

Every effort has been made to ensure the accuracy of information within this publication but the publishers cannot be held responsible for any errors or omissions. Views expressed are those of the author and do not necessarily represent those of the publishers or the football

CONTENTS

5   Welcome from Alan Pardew
6   2013/14 Season Review
14 2013/14 Season Statistics
15 Classic Clashes
16 Tyne and Wear Players
18 Player Q&As
20 Three of a Kind
21 NUFC Quiz
22 FA Cup and League Cup Reviews
23 French Quiz
24 Penalty Shoot-Outs
26 Behind the Scenes – Medical
28 Pre-Season
31 Joe Harvey
32 The Entertainers
35 United's New Boys

36 Reviews 1990s
37 Crossword
38 Reviews 2000s
39 Wordsearch
40 NUFC Roof Top Tours
42 Steve Harper Tribute
44 Player Quiz
45 The French Connection
46 United in the Community
49 Maths Challenge
50 Top Ten Goals 2013/14
54 United and the Great War
57 Spot the Difference
58 The Shola Files
60 Goal Celebrations
62 Quiz Answers

St. James' Park

WELCOME FROM
ALAN PARDEW

I am proud to once again be writing the introduction for the official 2015 Newcastle United Annual. I trust, as always, that you will enjoy reading this year's edition.

The 2013/14 season was an odd one to say the least. We started off very brightly and were up there with the top teams in the league around Christmas time, but the second half of the campaign was hugely disappointing as we let our standards slip and that simply wasn't good enough for a club of this standing.

We recruited well over the summer months and the players we brought to the club have added numbers to our squad, but more importantly, they have added quality and without a doubt that was the main ingredient I was looking for.

At Newcastle United we consider ourselves incredibly lucky to have some of the most passionate fans in the country, and without that amazing support, this club would not be the one that is renowned throughout the world of football. The atmosphere you generate inside the stadium gives the players such a huge lift so I thank you most sincerely for that.

In this year's annual I've particularly enjoyed reading about some of the great players we have had over the years and I hope too you'll enjoy the behind the scenes articles we have, which will give you an insight into what really happens at a Premier League football club.

Another highpoint was seeing a number of our players at the World Cup in Brazil last summer. What a tournament it was and what a fantastic job those players did for their nations. Not only did they make their countries proud but we as a club should feel very proud of them for also representing Newcastle United.

Enjoy the read and may I extend my very best wishes to you all.

Alan Pardew
Team Manager

A SEASON OF UPS AND DOWNS

The Magpies started the season well and up until the New Year, the team were playing good flowing football with results to match. '2014 proved to be a disappointment though, as the form nose-dived and the side struggled for goals. There was however, at times, much to applaud in the Premier League campaign including exciting victories over Chelsea at St. James' Park and well-earned wins at Tottenham and Manchester United. After September, The Magpies were never out of the top 10 with the final finishing position of tenth. Respectable but it could possibly have been a little bit higher.

AUGUST

After a promising pre-season, the unforgiving fixture generator handed Newcastle United a tough trip to Manchester City on the opening day of the 2013/14 Barclays Premier League season. The game at the Etihad Stadium brought about few positives for the Magpies, as goals from David Silva, Sergio Aguero, Yaya Toure and Samir Nasri condemned them to a 4-0 defeat.

However, Alan Pardew's side were boosted by the arrival of striker Loic Remy, on loan from QPR. Although Remy was unable to feature in the first three fixtures of the campaign due to injury, he did eventually make his bow as a 74th minute substitute in the 1-0 victory over Fulham at St. James' Park on the 31st August, a game which was decided by a moment of magic from Hatem Ben Arfa four minutes from time.

Earlier in the week, a United side featuring the likes of Rob Elliot, Gael Bigirimana and Curtis Good saw off the challenge of plucky League 2 outfit Morecambe in the Capital One Cup, with late strikes from the Ameobi brothers, Shola and Sammy, picking off the Shrimps at the Globe Arena.

Ending the month with four points from nine in the league, three clean sheets from four and progression in a domestic cup competition, it represented a decent August for Pardew's men, aside from the thumping defeat at the hands of the champions elect at Eastlands.

SEPTEMBER

After a two-week international break, Newcastle returned to action at Villa Park and it was Ben Arfa who, once again, found the target to give United the lead. Christian Benteke's equaliser came against the run of play, but with the ever-impressive Yohan Cabaye dictating the play, it was Yoan Gouffran who grabbed the winner, pouncing after Brad Guzan had parried into his path.

However, the following week brought about the Magpies' first loss at home of the campaign – a 3-2 reverse against newly-promoted Hull City. Loic Remy's first-half double – the first strikes of his loan spell – sandwiched a Robbie Brady goal to give the home side a narrow advantage at the break, but two goals after the break gave native Geordie Steve Bruce a welcome three points.

The Capital One Cup draw brought a tie that just 10 years ago would have been a top-half fixture in the Barclays Premier League, as Leeds United made the trip to St. James' Park. The visitors threatened sporadically, but Papiss Cisse and Gouffran again gave the Magpies victory.

Back in league action five days later, United went down 3-2 to a resurgent Everton. Led by the in-form duo of Romelu Lukaku and Ross Barkley, Roberto Martinez's Toffees found themselves three goals to the good before half time. A spectacular Yohan Cabaye strike got the Toon back into it, but a late Remy toe-poke proved to be little more than a consolation as they ended the month on a sour note.

OCTOBER

United kicked off October with a visit to South Wales to face Cardiff City – the first time the two clubs had met in the Premier League – and a brace from Remy was enough to earn United the points.

Next up was a daunting fixture at home to a revitalised Liverpool, who boasted the prolific duo of Luis Suarez and Daniel Sturridge up front. Yohan Cabaye broke the deadlock at St. James' Park, drilling home another long-range strike before Steven Gerrard tucked away a penalty to equalise. With Mapou Yanga-Mbiwa red-carded, ten-men United went ahead again though Paul Dummett's maiden goal for his hometown club, but the numerical disadvantage eventually told when Sturridge headed the leveller with under 20 minutes left on the clock.

Buoyed by two positive results, the Tyne-Wear derby looked to have come around at the right time for Newcastle. In front of over 46,000 at the Stadium of Light, Sunderland upset the form book as goals from Steven Fletcher and Fabio Borini gave the Wearsiders the points, with Mathieu Debuchy slotting in United's consolation.

Three days later, Manchester City were the opponents for the second time in under three months. Sadly, goals from Alvaro Negredo and Edin Dzeko in extra time at St. James' Park ended United's interest in the Capital One Cup.

NOVEMBER

Recording four wins out of four, November proved to be the perfect month for Newcastle United. An impressive 2-0 victory over Chelsea at home – sealed by a Yoan Gouffran header and a Loic Remy left-footer – set the tone.

Tottenham Hotspur were next up and it was Loic Remy – again – who won the game. It would be unfair, however, to overlook the contribution of goalkeeper Tim Krul in this victory. The number one pulled off a string of fantastic saves to keep Spurs at bay, and the Dutchman's fine performance complemented a resolute, solid display from his team.

Remy was on the scoresheet again against Norwich City on the 23rd November, heading home Yohan

Cabaye's corner after just 115 seconds for his eighth of the season. Yoan Gouffran added a second later in the half, prodding Shola Ameobi's goalbound header past John Ruddy. Though Leroy Fer pulled a goal back for ex-Toon boss Chris Hughton's struggling Canaries, it seemed nothing could stop Newcastle's march up the table this month.

And so it proved. West Bromwich Albion were the next side to be dispatched, as Moussa Sissoko's screamer, coupled with another Gouffran header, rendered Chris Brunt's second-half consolation meaningless. It was a 100% record for November, which helped Alan Pardew and Tim Krul win the Barclays Manager and Player of the Month awards respectively.

DECEMBER

United's impressive run of form came to an abrupt halt at the Liberty Stadium. Goals from Nathan Dyer and Jonjo Shelvey, either side of Mathieu Debuchy putting through his own net, saw Newcastle concede three for the first time since September's defeat at Everton and go down 3-0 in the process.

Three days later however, Alan Pardew and his side got back to winning ways in style. A trip to Old Trafford to play Manchester United was made no less daunting by the fact that the Magpies hadn't won at the famous old ground since February 1972 – some 41 years earlier. Moussa Sissoko got the better of another Frenchman, Patrice Evra, down the right and squared for the classy Cabaye, who arrived in the box at the perfect time to sweep past David de Gea, giving the 3,000-strong travelling Toon

Army their first taste of victory in the red half of Manchester in 33 attempts.

That brilliant result away from home was followed by an encouraging 1-1 draw with Southampton back at St. James' Park, where Jay Rodriguez levelled for the Saints after Yoan Gouffran's opener.

United's final pre-Christmas fixture saw them take on Crystal Palace at Selhurst Park. Yohan Cabaye, Palace stopper Danny Gabbidon and Hatem Ben Arfa all slotted past Julian Speroni to hand the visitors a convincing 3-0 win. A thumping 5-1 home win over Stoke City followed on Boxing Day, the visitors finishing with just nine men before the four-game unbeaten run came to an end at the hands of Arsenal.

JANUARY

Saido Berahino, the young West Brom forward, denied Newcastle a winning start to 2014 by scoring an 87th-minute penalty at the Hawthorns. Tim Krul was adjudged to have brought down Matej Vydra in the closing stages, allowing Berahino to stroke home the winner.

Things got no better that weekend, as Cardiff City put an end to any hopes of a domestic cup run with a 2-1 victory in the third round of the FA Cup. Papiss Cisse's 62nd-minute strike was cancelled out by Craig Noone and, with just 10 minutes remaining, Fraizer Campbell struck to heap misery on the 31,166 fans inside St. James' Park.

A rampant Manchester City then made it four straight defeats in all competitions with a 2-0 win at St. James' Park – Edin Dzeko and Alvaro Negredo the scorers – in a game that was notable for a disallowed Cheick Tiote thunderbolt. The Ivorian's left-footed half-volley flew past Joe Hart into the corner but Yoan Gouffran, who was in close proximity to the England goalkeeper, was controversially deemed to have interfered with play in an offside position.

Yohan Cabaye's double and another goal from Loic Remy handed United a 3-1 win at Upton Park before a 0-0 draw at Norwich City followed, but the point came at a price as Remy was sent off following an altercation with Bradley Johnson.

FEBRUARY

February began in miserable fashion for United. A 3-0 defeat at the hands of Sunderland in the Tyne-Wear derby meant that Newcastle had now failed to win a derby since 2011's 1-0 win at the Stadium of Light, courtesy of Ryan Taylor's free-kick. Fabio Borini, Adam Johnson and Jack Colback scored the goals that stuck the knife into the Magpies in front of their own support.

Newcastle were on the end of another 3-0 drubbing a week later, this time at the hands of Jose Mourinho's Chelsea. Eden Hazard inspired his side to victory, netting a hat-trick to wrap up three well-deserved points for the Blues.

To further compound the misery, Tottenham Hotspur managed to grab four goals at St. James' next time out — a double from Emmanuel Adebayor and one each from Paulinho and Nacer Chadli — to make the form guide grim reading for Toon fans.

The month was to end on a high note, though, as Aston Villa were dispatched in front of over 50,000 on Tyneside. Loic Remy's stoppage-time strike was enough to scrape past the Midlanders, who proved stubborn opponents before Remy rattled home the winner, twisting and turning his way away from the Villa backline to smash home at the Gallowgate End and stop the rot.

MARCH

Fresh from the morale-boosting win at the end of February, Newcastle went to Hull in good spirits. Moussa Sissoko's double added to a goal from Loic Remy and Vurnon Anita's first league goal sealed an impressive 4-1 win at the KC, rendering Curtis Davies' header irrelevant. The emphatic win was marred by a touchline altercation involving Alan Pardew which led to the Newcastle manager receiving a five-match stadium ban and a further three-match touchline ban, in addition to a heavy fine.

With John Carver leading the team from the touchline, a visit to Craven Cottage to face lowly Fulham was up next, but Algerian international Ashkan Dejagah's well struck shot gave the Cottagers victory in the game 17-year-old Academy graduate Adam Armstrong came off the bench to make his League debut.

Tony Pulis had presided over an upsurge in form since stepping into the Crystal Palace hotseat and their top-flight status was almost certainly secured. It took a last-gasp header from Papiss Cisse to finally break the deadlock and grab all three points.

With just eight league fixtures remaining, form and luck was to desert Alan Pardew's men. A 3-0 midweek home defeat against an impressive Everton outfit opened the floodgates for a disastrous run of form, which saw six games pass without recording a victory. Southampton's international frontline of Rickie Lambert, Jay Rodriguez and Adam Lallana were next to shoot down Newcastle, with a 4-0 defeat at the end of the month.

APRIL

With Manchester United next up, there looked to be no easy route back to form. Juan Mata, a £37 million signing from Chelsea in the January transfer window, pulled the strings all afternoon and netted the first with a brilliant, curling free-kick. Another from Mata made it two, before Javier Hernandez and Adnan Januzaj added extra gloss to the scoreline.

Stoke City is traditionally an unwelcoming arena for visiting players, and so it proved once more on the 12th April. Erik Pieters' looping cross beat Tim Krul's outstretched arm to give the Potters a fluke lead and ultimately, the points.

Another team not enjoying the greatest of runs were Swansea City. Shola Ameobi put Newcastle ahead, slotting past Michel Vorm, but Wilfried Bony, City's prolific record signing, headed the Welshmen level on the stroke of half-time, before Cheick Tiote's challenge on Marvin Emnes at the death allowed his fellow Ivorian to win it with an emphatic spot-kick.

After four successive defeats, a trip to the Emirates Stadium to face Arsenal wasn't the most enticing prospect. A 3-0 defeat was probably a fair reflection of proceedings with Laurent Koscielny, Mesut Ozil and Olivier Giroud all on target.

MAY

Finally, a win – and a convincing one at that. In a game which saw Ole Gunnar Solskjaer's Bluebirds relegated, Shola Ameobi headed United in front with what turned out to be his final goal, number 79 in total, for his hometown club in his last home game. Fitting too that he should score it at the Gallowgate End. Late goals from Loic Remy, also appearing in black and white for the final time, and Steven Taylor, his first for nearly three years, sealed a 3-0 win amidst a palpable feeling of relief at St. James' Park.

The final day fixture at Liverpool ended in a 2-1 defeat, with Ameobi and Paul Dummett both seeing red. It was a sad way for Shola to finish his career on Tyneside but at least he had the consolation of heading off to Brazil for the World Cup with Nigeria, the country of his birth. Liverpool could have won that title that day but needed West Ham to win at the Etihad, something that realistically was never going to happen, after the Reds had lost at home to Chelsea two weeks earlier with the title in their grasp.

So it was a 10th-place finish in the Barclays Premier League for United, which could have been ninth if Charlie Adam hadn't struck a very late winner for Stoke at West Brom, which represented a solid if unspectacular season for the Magpies, with plenty of positives to take into the 2014/15 season.

SEASON STATISTICS

	League	FA Cup	Lge Cup	2013/14	Total NUFC
Sammy AMEOBI	4 (6) 0	0 (0) 0	2 (0) 1	6 (6) 1	13 (27) 2
Shola AMEOBI	14 (12) 2	0 (1) 0	1 (1) 1	15 (14) 3	219 (178) 79
Vurnon ANITA	28 (6) 1	1 (0) 0	2 (0) 0	31 (6) 1	58 (16) 2
Adam ARMSTRONG	0 (4) 0	0 (0) 0	0 (0) 0	0 (4) 0	0 (4) 0
Hatem BEN ARFA	13 (14) 3	1 (0) 0	0 (2) 0	14 (16) 3	55 (31) 14
Gael BIGIRIMANA	0 (0) 0	0 (0) 0	1 (0) 0	1 (0) 0	13 (13) 10
Papiss CISSE	15 (9) 2	1 (0) 1	2 (0) 1	18 (9) 4	75 (13) 30
Yohan CABAYE	15 (2) 7	0 (0) 0	0 (1) 0	15 (3) 7	85 (6) 17
Fabricio COLOCCINI	27 (0) 0	0 (0) 0	1 (0) 0	28 (0) 0	210 (2) 5
Mathieu DEBUCHY	28 (1) 1	0 (0) 0	3 (0) 0	31 (1) 1	45 (1) 1
Luke DE JONG	8 (4) 0	0 (0) 0	0 (0) 0	0 (0) 0	8 (4) 0
Paul DUMMETT	11 (7) 1	0 (0) 0	2 (1) 0	13 (8) 1	13 (9) 1
Rob ELLIOT	2 (0) 0	1 (0) 0	1 (0) 0	4 (0) 0	21 (1) 0
Curtis GOOD	0 (0) 0	0 (0) 0	1 (0) 0	1 (0) 0	1 (0) 0
Dan GOSLING	4 (4) 0	0 (0) 0	1 (1) 0	5 (5) 0	12 (24) 1
Yoan GOUFFRAN	31 (4) 6	1 (0) 0	3 (0) 1	35 (4) 7	49 (5) 10
Jonas GUTIERREZ	1 (1) 0	0 (0) 0	0 (0) 0	1 (1) 0	174 (21) 11
Massadio HAIDARA	3 (8) 0	1 (0) 0	1 (0) 0	5 (8) 0	11 (10) 0
Tim KRUL	36 (0) 0	0 (0) 0	2 (0) 0	38 (0) 0	142 (3) 0
Sylvain MARVEAUX	2 (7) 0	0 (0) 0	2 (0) 0	4 (7) 0	28 (29) 2
Gabriel OBERTAN	0 (3) 0	0 (1) 0	0 (1) 0	0 (5) 0	33 (22) 2
Loic REMY	24 (2) 14	0 (0) 0	0 (0) 0	24 (2) 14	24 (2) 14
Davide SANTON	26 (1) 0	1 (0) 0	0 (0) 0	27 (1) 0	87 (6) 1
Moussa SISSOKO	35 (0) 3	1 (0) 0	1 (1) 0	37 (1) 3	55 (1) 6
Steven TAYLOR	9 (1) 1	1 (0) 0	0 (0) 0	10 (1) 1	228 (18) 14
Cheick TIOTE	31 (2) 0	1 (0) 0	2 (0) 0	34 (2) 0	112 (7) 1
Haris VUCKIC	0 (0) 0	0 (0) 0	1 (1) 0	1 (1) 0	9 (8) 1
Mike WILLIAMSON	32 (1) 0	0 (0) 0	2 (0) 0	34 (1) 0	132 (4) 0
Mapou YANGA-MBIWA	17 (6) 0	1 (0) 0	2 (0) 0	20 (6) 0	37 (9) 0

CLASSIC CLASHES

Newcastle United have been involved in many memorable and outstanding matches in their history. Some are labelled 'great' because of the excitement generated, some by their significance and some by the terrific football played and quality of the goals scored. In this annual we go back to the 2001/02 season when United went top of the Premier League after a fantastic 3-1 midweek win at Highbury.

DECEMBER 18TH 2001
PREMIER LEAGUE
ARSENAL 1 - NEWCASTLE UNITED 3

Andy O'Brien, Alan Shearer and Laurent Robert scored the goals that not only ended the London hoodoo (United hadn't won in the capital for 29 games) but put the Magpies at the top of the League.

It was a crazy night at Highbury which had no hint of Geordie glory when a rampant Arsenal took the lead on 20 minutes in a devastating opening half hour. Thierry Henry juggled the ball and crossed to Robert Pires who appeared to handle before the ball was squared back to him to tap in from close range.

But the game turned before half-time, when Ray Parlour was sent off for his second yellow card as he challenged Shearer from behind. United were back in it on the hour when a near post corner from Lomana LuaLua was headed home by a jubilant Andy O'Brien in front of the Toon fans, with the home defence standing motionless.

Craig Bellamy was then red carded after catching Ashley Cole in the face and it was all level again. Into the final 10 minutes it was anyone's game, but thankfully it was the visitors who struck. On 86

Laurent Robert clinches the three points

minutes, Alan Shearer calmly dispatched a penalty past Stuart Taylor, with Arsenal still grumbling about a dubious spot kick award resulting from the challenge of Sol Campbell on Laurent Robert. Bobby Robson's men wrapped it up right at the death when a LuaLua pass let in a galloping Robert who cracked the ball in for the third and confirmed United's ascendancy to the summit of the Premier League.

An elated Manager Bobby Robson said:

"It's an amazing feeling, we've done it, we've won in London and we've gone top of the league.

"I thought Arsenal were mesmeric in the first half and there was a gulf in class between the two teams.

"We showed great resilience and character in the second half and I can't tell you how happy and proud I am."

UNITED: Given; Hughes, Elliott (Robert); Dabizas, O'Brien, Speed; Solano (LuaLua), Dyer (Distin), Shearer, Bellamy, Bernard

GOALS: United: O'Brien 60, Shearer pen 86, Robert 90. Arsenal: Henry 20

ATTENDANCE: 38,012

Alan Shearer puts United ahead from the spot

TYNE — WEAR MAGPIES

With Jack Colback having joined the Magpies in the close season from local rivals Sunderland, we take a look here at those players who have played for both North East clubs. Below is the full list, alphabetically, with appearance/goals listed in brackets after the time spent at St. James' Park.

	Newcastle	Sunderland
William Agnew	1902-04 (44/0)	1908-10
Stan Anderson	1963-65 (84/14)	1951-63
John Auld	1896-06 (15/3)	1889–96
Harry Bedford	1930-32 (32/18)	1932-33
Paul Bracewell	1992-95 (87/4)	1989-92
Ivor Broadis	1953-55 (51/18)	1949-51
Michael Bridges	2004 (9/0)	1995-99
Alan Brown	1981-82 (5/3)	1976-82

Michael Chopra

Lee Clark

Titus Bramble

	Newcastle	Sunderland
Titus Bramble	2002-07 (157/7)	2010-13
Steve Caldwell	2000-04 (37/2)	2004-07
Michael Chopra	2002-06 (31/3)	2007-09
Lee Clark	1988-97 & 04-05 (265/28)	1997-99
Johnny Campbell	1897-98 (29/12)	1889-97
Jeff Clarke	1982-86 (134/5)	1975-82
Andy Cole	1993-95 (84/68)	2007-08
Joe Devine	1930-31 (22/11)	1931-33
John Dowsey	1924-26 (3/0)	1927-29
Ray Ellison	1968-73 (7/0)	1973-74
Robbie Elliott	1989-97 & 01-06 (188/12)	2006-07
Alan Foggon	1965-71 (80/16)	1976-77
Howard Gayle	1982-83 (8/2)	1984-86
Thomas Grey	1908-10 (1/0)	
Ron Guthrie	1963-73 (66/2)	1973-75

Ivor Broadis

John Harvey

Len Shackleton

	Newcastle	Sunderland
Bob Thomson	1928-34 (80/0)	1927-28
Thomas Urwin	1924-30 (200/24)	1930-34
Barry Venison	1992-95 (133/1)	1979-86
Chris Waddle	1980-85 (191/52)	1997 (7/1)
Nigel Walker	1977-82 (74/3)	1982-83
Billy Whitehurst	1985-86 (31/7)	1988
Dave Willis	1907-13 (108/4)	1904-97
David Young	1964-73 (56/2)	1973-74

Furthermore, in the Premier League era, Colback is the eighth to play for both clubs:

- Paul Bracewell, Newcastle United 48 games, Sunderland 38
- Titus Bramble, Newcastle United 105 games, Sunderland 47
- Michael Bridges Newcastle United 6 games, Sunderland 25
- Steve Caldwell, Newcastle United 26 games, Sunderland 24
- Michael Chopra, Newcastle United 21 games, Sunderland 39
- Andy Cole, Newcastle United 58 games, Sunderland 7
- Louis Saha, Newcastle United 11 games Sunderland 11

Incidentally, Lee Clark and Robbie Elliott, who also played for both clubs recently, aren't included in the above list as their football at Sunderland was played whilst the Black Cats were in the Championship. Chris Waddle, on the other hand, played his top-flight football at Newcastle before the introduction of the Premier League. Furthermore, Lionel Perez is not included on any list as he didn't play first team football at St. James' Park.

In addition, there are others with recent links between the two clubs: Sam Allardyce played for Sunderland in the early 1980s before managing United in 2007/08, Bob Stokoe won the FA Cup as a player for United in 1955 and repeated that as manager at Roker Park in 1973 whilst Stokoe's assistant that day, Arthur Cox, went on to manage United from 1982-84.

	Newcastle	Sunderland
Tom Hall	1913-20 (58/16)	1909-13
Tommy Gibb	1968-75 (268/19)	1975-77
Shay Given	1997-09 (463/0)	1996
Steve Hardwick	1976-83 (101/0)	1987-88
Mick Harford	1980-81 (19/4)	1993
John Harvey	1897-1900 (35/10)	1892-97
David Kelly	1991-93 (83/39)	1995
Alan Kennedy	1971-78 (216/10)	1985-87
James Logan	1895-96 (9/8)	1891-92
Bob McDermid	1894-97 (64/2)	1888-90
Andy McCombie	1904-10 (131/0)	1898-04
Bob McKay	1926-28 (66/23)	1928-30
Albert McInroy	1929-34 (160/0)	1934-35
Jackie Milburn	1943-57 (397/200)	1944-45
Bob Moncur	1960-74 (361/10)	1974-76
James Raine	1905-06 (4/1)	1906-08
Bobby Robinson	1952-54 (5/0)	1947-52
Ray Robinson	1919-20 (29/4)	1920-21
Bryan Robson	1962-71 (244/97)	1974-76
Tom Rowlandson	1905-06 (1/0)	1903-05
Louis Saha	1999 (12/2)	2012-13
Len Shackleton	1946-48 (64/29)	1948-58
Jock Smith	1894-96 (27/10)	1889-93
Colin Suggett	1978-81 (24/0)	1964-66
Ernie Taylor	1942-51 (117/21)	1958-61

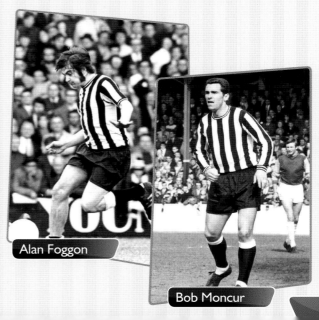

Alan Foggon

Bob Moncur

Ryan Taylor

Boyhood hero?	David Beckham
Best footballing moment?	Scoring the winner from a free kick at the Stadium of Light in August 2011
Team supported as a boy?	Liverpool
Pre Match meal?	Chicken and Pasta
Any superstitions?	Right boot on first!
Favourite current player?	Ronaldo
Favourite other sports person?	LeBron James
Favourite stadium other than St. James' Park?	Anfield
Favourite food?	Italian
What would you be if you weren't a footballer?	A fireman
Where did you go for your 2014 summer holiday?	Las Vegas
Favourite actor?	Denzel Washington
What do you like doing in your spare time?	Spending time with my family
Which three people would you invite round for dinner?	David Beckham, Robert De Niro and Michael Jordan

Jack Colback

Boyhood hero?	Alan Shearer
Best footballing moment?	Playing in a Wembley Cup Final in 2014
Team supported as a boy?	Newcastle United
Pre Match meal?	Pasta
Any superstitions?	None
Favourite current player?	Xavi
Favourite other sports person?	Floyd Mayweather
Favourite stadium other than St. James' Park?	Old Trafford
Favourite food?	Sunday lunch
What would you be if you weren't a footballer?	Maybe a groundsman
Where did you go for your 2014 summer holiday?	Portugal
Favourite actor?	Johnny Depp
What do you like doing in your spare time?	Being with my family
Which three people would you invite round for dinner?	Kevin Bridges, Roger Federer and Karl Pilkington

Vurnon Anita

Boyhood hero?	
Edgar Davids	
Best footballing moment?	
Signing my first professional contract at Ajax on my 16th birthday	
Team supported as a boy?	
Ajax	
Pre Match meal?	
Spaghetti	
Any superstitions?	
No	
Favourite current player?	
Andres Iniesta	
Favourite other sports person?	
LeBron James	
Favourite stadium other than St. James' Park?	
Ajax Arena	
Favourite food?	
Bonchi	
What would you be if you weren't a footballer?	
In the sports clothing business	
Where did you go for your 2014 summer holiday?	
Curacao (Caribbean Sea Island)	
Favourite actor?	
Denzel Washington	
What do you like doing in your spare time?	
Being with my wife and children	
Which three people would you invite round for dinner?	
Drake, LeBron James and Andres Iniesta	

Fabricio Coloccini

Boyhood hero?	
Diego Maradona	
Best footballing moment?	
Winning Gold at the 2004 Olympic Games	
Team supported as a boy?	
San Lorenzo (Argentina)	
Pre Match meal?	
Spaghetti	
Any superstitions?	
None	
Favourite current player?	
Lionel Messi	
Favourite other sports person?	
I admire many throughout sport	
Favourite stadium other than St. James' Park?	
Old Trafford	
Favourite food?	
Spaghetti/Pasta	
What would you be if you weren't a footballer?	
A pilot	
Where did you go for your 2014 summer holiday?	
Argentina	
Favourite actor?	
Ricardo Darin	
What do you like doing in your spare time?	
I like my music very much	
Which three people would you invite round for dinner?	
Alex Ferguson, Marcelo Bielsa and Cristina Fernandez de Kirchner (President of Argentina)	

THREE OF A KIND

1 Three players who are Italian to have played for United?

....

....

....

2 Three players to score over 150 goals for the Club?

....

....

....

3 Three players who have scored Premier League hat-tricks for United in the 1990s?

....

....

....

4 Three players to have played over 400 League games for the Toon?

....

....

5 Three managers from the 1960s?

....

....

....

6 Three teams United have scored six against in the Premier League?

....

....

....

7 From the answers to questions 1 to 6, which three players have played in the World Cup Finals?

....

....

....

8 From the answers to questions 1 to 6, which three players also played for Manchester United?

....

....

....

ANSWERS ON PAGE 62

WHAT DO YOU REMEMBER ABOUT THE 2013/14 SEASON?

1. Who scored United's last goal of 2013?

2. Who knocked United out of the FA Cup?

3. Which two teams scored the most goals against United?

4. Yoan Gouffran scored in how many consecutive home games in November and December?

5. Which United player was sent off on New Year's Day?

6. United won at Old Trafford for the first time since which season?

7. Loic Remy joined from QPR but which French club did he play for previously?

8. Which two teams did United fail to score against last season?

9. Who debuted in the League Cup for United but is yet to play in the Premier League?

10. Who were the only three players to score more than once in the same game?

SEE HOW MUCH YOU KNOW ABOUT NEWCASTLE UNITED PAST AND PRESENT!

1. In which year did Newcastle infamously lose to Hereford in the FA Cup?

2. Who was manager for Newcastle's first Premier League game in 1993?

3. Alan Shearer, David Batty and Craig Bellamy all have connections with which other team?

4. In 1924, did United compete in the first, second or third FA Cup Final at the new Wembley Stadium?

5. Who were United's first FA Cup Final opponents in 1905?

6. Where did United clinch promotion to the Premier League in May 1993?

7. Which team did United beat in the semi-finals to reach Wembley in 1974?

8. Which Italian club did Paul Gascoigne play for?

9. Which two teams have United scored seven against in the Premier League?

10. Who is the only Norwegian to play for United in the Premier League?

ANSWERS ON PAGE 62

21

FA CUP AND LEAGUE CUP REVIEWS

FA CUP ROUND UP

Rd 3: Newcastle 1–2 Cardiff

The FA Cup is a competition which is famous around the world and when the final comes around in May, it is one of the most celebrated days in English football. Newcastle last won the cup in 1955 against Manchester City and have been beaten in three finals since then; 1974 against Liverpool, 1998 against Arsenal, and 1999 against Manchester United.

Newcastle drew Cardiff City in the third round at home, and the Reds, who were formally the Blues, had a new manager at the helm, the baby-faced assassin, ex Manchester United striker Ole Gunnar Solskjaer. The Bluebirds hadn't beaten Newcastle at St James' Park in over 50 years, but unfortunately that was all about to change.

Newcastle took the game to Cardiff and were unlucky not to be ahead when Hatem Ben Arfa hit the woodwork either side of the interval. United eventually went ahead when Papiss Cisse scored in the 61st minute, and that should have been that. The Geordies were shocked though, when an amazing 30 yard strike from substitute Craig Noone leveled things up, and it was another substitute, Fraizer Campbell, who got the second when he headed past Rob Elliot in the 80th minute. The game ended 2-1 to Cardiff and that's where, sadly, Newcastle's 2013/14 cup campaign ended.

LEAGUE CUP ROUND UP

Rd 2: Morecambe 0–2 Newcastle United
Rd 3: Newcastle United 2–0 Leeds United
Rd 4: Newcastle United 0–2 Manchester City

Newcastle United do not have fond memories of the League Cup, having only managed to reach the final on one occasion in its 53 year history, losing to Manchester City in 1976. Although there was no success in this year's competition, Newcastle could hold their heads higher than the previous year, losing only after extra time to the eventual League Cup winners and Premier League champions, Manchester City.

The Magpies started the tournament in round 2 with a trip away to Morecambe at the Globe Arena. Newcastle fielded a changed side which included the likes of Gael Bigirimana, Dan Gosling, and making his only appearance of the season, Curtis Good. It was the Ameobi brothers who got the goals though, with both Sammy and Shola netting in the last 10 minutes to give Newcastle a 2-0 win, which confirmed progression into round 3.

Up next were Leeds United, who were the visitors at St James' Park. Papiss Cisse gave Newcastle the lead in the first half, with a bullet like header which flew past the Leeds keeper Paddy Kenny. Newcastle doubled their lead in the second half with a goal from Yoan Gouffran, who turned his marker well on the edge of the area before firing the ball hard into the Gallowgate goal. It was a superb goal from the Frenchman and another 2-0 win for the Toon.

The draw was not kind to Newcastle as they pulled out Manchester City in the 4th round, but Alan Pardew's men gave it a good go and were unlucky not to be leading when Shola Ameobi had a shot saved well by Pantilimon during normal time. The 90 minutes ended 0-0 and as customary in the League Cup, the game went to extra time. Newcastle's resolve was broken in the 99th minute when Alvaro Negredo tucked in a cross from Edin Dzeko. It was then Dzeko himself who managed to get round Tim Krul to score, finishing off a very slick move from City.

FRENCH QUIZ

What is this...? Qu'est-ce que c'est...?

1
- **a** Les baskets
- **b** Les crampons
- **c** Les pantoufles
- **d** Les chaussettes

2
- **a** Le filet
- **b** Le poteau de but
- **c** La surface de réparation
- **d** Le poteau de corner

3
- **a** Un journal
- **b** Un magazine
- **c** Un programme
- **d** Un livre

4
- **a** Un t-shirt
- **b** Le pantalon
- **c** Un survêtement
- **d** Le maillot des Bleus

FRANCE

5
- **a** Carton jaune
- **b** Carton rouge
- **c** Maillot jaune
- **d** Arbite

ANSWERS ON PAGE 62

PENALTY SHOOT-OUTS

If you think England aren't the greatest at winning penalty shoot-outs, then Newcastle United run them pretty close, with just one success out of eight competitive attempts.

THE FULL RECORD READS

	Competitive	Minor Cups/ Friendly	Total
Shoot-Outs	8	13	21
Won	1	6	7
Lost	7	6	13
Draw		1	1

That came in a League Cup tie at Vicarage Road, Watford, in November 2006 when United beat their hosts 5–4 on spot-kicks, with keeper Steve Harper saving the vital kick from Jordan Stewart.

United were first involved in a penalty shoot-out competition in the 1970/71 Inter Cities Fairs Cup campaign, since then, in competitive football, i.e. FA Cup, League Cup and European competitions, the record is 'played' eight, won one and lost seven (and six of the eight have been at St. James' Park).

United have managed to win five friendly/minor cup penalty competitions, and at the same time lose six such shoot-outs. Bizarrely, there's also been a draw…

Ecstatic: Steve Harper after making the crucial save at Watford.

COMPETITIVE MATCHES

1970/71
Competition	Inter Cities Fairs Cup
Final Score	Pecsi Dozsa 2–2 Newcastle
Venue	Pecs
Penalties	Pecsi Dozsa 3–0 Newcastle
Scored	(McFaul & Clark did score 4 & 5)
Missed	Robson, Mitchell, Gibb

1979/80
Competition	Football League Cup
Final Score	Newcastle 2–2 Sunderland
Venue	St. James' Park
Penalties	Newcastle 6-7 Sunderland
Scored	Shoulder, Withe, Martin, Davies Barton, Brownlie
Missed	Pearson

1991/92
Competition	FA Cup
Final Score	Newcastle 2–2 Bournemouth
Venue	St. James' Park
Penalties	Newcastle 3–4 Bournemouth
Scored	Peacock, Watson, Appleby
Missed	O'Brien, Brock

1995/96
Competition	FA Cup
Final Score	Newcastle 2–2 Chelsea
Venue	St. James' Park
Penalties	Newcastle 2 – 4 Chelsea
Scored	Beresford, Albert
Missed	Beardsley, Watson

1998/99

Competition	Football League Cup
Final Score	Newcastle 1–1 Blackburn
Venue	St. James' Park
Penalties	Newcastle 2–4 Blackburn
Scored	Shearer, Pearce
Missed	Hamann, Hughes

2002/03

Competition	Football League Cup
Final Score	Newcastle 3–3 Everton
Venue	St. James' Park
Penalties	Newcastle 2–3 Everton
Scored	Dyer, Solano
Missed	Viana, Chopra, Robert

Sadly Big Al's penalty is heading over the bar…

2003/04

Competition	Champions League Qualifying Rd
Final Score	Newcastle 1–1 Partizan Belgrade
Venue	St. James' Park
Penalties	Newcastle 3–4 Partizan
Scored	Ameobi, LuaLua, Jenas
Missed	Shearer, Dyer, Woodgate, Hughes

2006/07

Competition	Football League Cup
Final Score	Watford 2–2 Newcastle
Venue	Vicarage Road
Penalties	Newcastle 5-4 Watford
Scored	Solano, Emre, Duff, Carr, N'Zogbia
Missed	Milner

Devastated: Aaron Hughes has just missed against Partizan Belgrade in the Champions League

FRIENDLY MATCHES

1971/72	Texaco Cup	Newcastle 4–3 Hearts
1982/83	Madeira Cup	Newcastle 1–4 Nacional
1987/88	Mercantile Credit Tournament	Newcastle 1–0 Liverpool
1991/92	Zenith Data Systems Cup	Tranmere 3–2 Newcastle
1994/95	Ibrox Tournament	Newcastle 6–5 Manchester United
1997/98	Umbro Tournament	Newcastle 1–3 Chelsea
1998/99	JD Sports Cup	Newcastle 3–4 Benfica
1998/99	JD Sports Cup	Newcastle 4–3 Middlesbrough
2003/04	Premier League Asia Cup	Newcastle 4–5 Chelsea
2004/05	Far East Tour	Newcastle 2–4 Thailand XI
2004/05	The United Christian Medical Service Charity Challenge Cup	Newcastle 7–6 Kitchee
2010/11	Friendly	Newcastle 5–3 Deportivo
2012/13	XII Trofeo Guadiana	Newcastle 4–4 Olympiakos

BEHIND THE SCENES

Even in the old days, before a transfer was completed, players had to undergo a medical before they could join a new club. Tests carried out, even as far back as the 1970s were fairly basic. They are designed to ensure that players aren't carrying long term injuries, like a knee ligament problem for example. In the modern game, however, the medical is far more stringent, and players have to go through an exhaustive and comprehensive series of tests before they're able to sign on the dotted line for the Magpies. Our pictures show a range of tests that Frenchman Massadio Haidara underwent before his move to United from Nancy in January 2013.

Here he is just off the plane from France arriving for the first time at United's Benton training base with his representatives.

It's then into the gymnasium for a few running exercises and general fitness tests.

Massadio is pictured here with one of United's performance analysts, Jamie Harley.

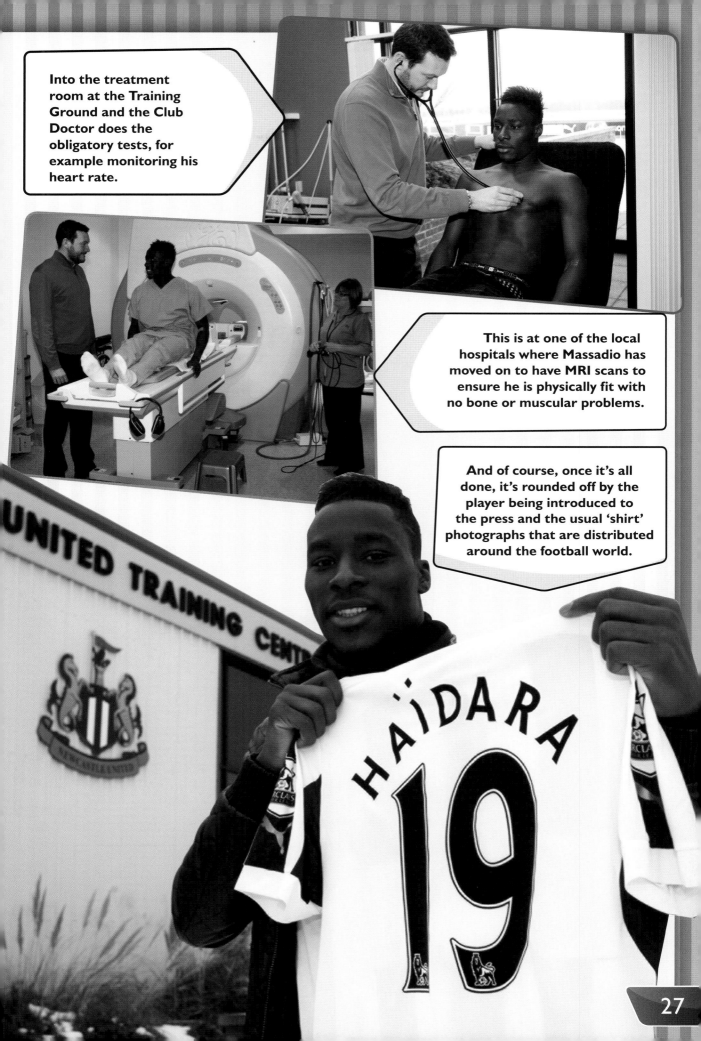

Into the treatment room at the Training Ground and the Club Doctor does the obligatory tests, for example monitoring his heart rate.

This is at one of the local hospitals where Massadio has moved on to have MRI scans to ensure he is physically fit with no bone or muscular problems.

And of course, once it's all done, it's rounded off by the player being introduced to the press and the usual 'shirt' photographs that are distributed around the football world.

Pre-season is traditionally a tough time for the players, but at Newcastle United, new Head of Fitness Dave Billows, who was formerly with Everton, tries to make it as much fun as possible whilst still ensuring that the serious business of getting fit for the new season remains top of the agenda. In our picture selection here we see the players doing various drills on their first day back at work in early July, as the build up for the Premier League season in August began in earnest.

The pitchside barriers come in handy for loosening up.

It's a gentle limber up for the lads, led by Dave Billows, before the more intensive fitness work starts.

In days gone by you may not have seen a ball on the first day of training, it was all running, but here Siem De Jong shows modern training methods have moved on from simply clocking up the miles!

Masseur Wayne Farrage gets to grips with Mehdi Abeid.

Ryan Taylor and Massadio Haidara complete a shuttle drill designed to improve both strength and speed.

It's a bit faster this one, with longer running to get the aerobic conditioning of the players up to speed.

Paul Dummett leads the sub-maximal running exercise, watched closely by fitness coach Simon Tweddle. The players wear heart monitors and GB units so that the physical analysts can monitor performance levels.

Flexibility is a key part of a player's fitness programme, and here we see the squad getting put through their stretches.

The session is over and it's time for a cool down in the ice baths which helps muscle recovery after a hard workout.

A nice change for the lads as they stretch their legs on Longsands beach at nearby Tynemouth.

JOE, JOE, JOE HARVEY

Some of the greats of Newcastle United from the 1950s, 60s and 70s were back at St. James' Park last April to unveil a permanent memorial to the man who led the club to FA Cup and Fairs Cup triumphs – legendary Magpies captain and manager Joe Harvey, or as the popular terrace chant went, "Joe, Joe, Joe Harvey".

Harvey's son Ken, Fairs Cup winning captain Bob Moncur and Vic Keeble – the only surviving member of the 1955 cup-winning side of which Harvey was trainer, unveiled a huge 5ft x 3ft bronze plaque in his honour at the Gallowgate End of the ground, close to the statue of his former teammate, Jackie Milburn.

They were joined by Harvey's family and a host of famous ex-players including Wyn Davies, Frank Clark, Malcolm Macdonald, David Craig, Alan Foggon and Dave Hilley, as well the Fairs Club group which spearheaded the project with the support of fundraisers including Newcastle United, who made a significant donation and also paid for all installation costs.

As part of the ceremony, it was also announced that Joe Harvey has been inducted to the Newcastle United Foundation's Hall of Fame, joining revered club figures including Hughie Gallacher, Jackie Milburn, Bob Moncur, Sir Bobby Robson, Peter Beardsley and Alan Shearer. A trophy was presented by Bob Moncur to Ken Harvey to mark his father's induction.

A half-back as a player, Harvey captained the Magpies to promotion from the second tier in 1948 and successive FA Cup victories at Wembley in 1951 and 1952, returning to Wembley as the team's trainer for the club's third FA Cup success in five years in 1955.

He was appointed as Newcastle United manager in 1962 and after guiding the club to the Second Division title and promotion in 1965, he led the team to the Inter-Cities Fairs Cup – the pre-cursor to the UEFA Cup (now the UEFA Europe League) – in 1969 courtesy of a 6-2 aggregate victory over Hungarian side Ujpest Dozsa. It remains the club's most recent piece of major silverware.

After leading the club to another FA Cup Final in 1974, finishing as runners-up to Liverpool, Harvey remained as manager until the following season before loyally fulfilling a backroom role for the club. He passed away in Newcastle following a heart attack in February 1989.

Newcastle United supporters are passionate about their football. Aside from winning, of course, they love to be entertained too. They like their local lads and grafters too, but it's the players who give them that special buzz and raise the hairs on the back of their neck when they gain possession – they are the special ones. Here we capture some of those extraordinary talents from three eras, the pre 1960s, the 70s & 80s and finally, the 90s & 2000s. There are a few famous names who could easily earn a place on these pages too; star names such as Tino Asprilla, Tony Green and Malcolm Macdonald to name but three – United fans have certainly been blessed with many a character over the years.

JIMMY HOWIE (1903-1910)

Recognised in the game as one of the finest inside forwards of the era. From Scotland, he was known as 'Gentleman Jim' and oozed finesse. A genius at creating openings, Howie was a distinctive player and often thrilled the crowd with a celebrated dribble in which he went past defenders at ease. Capped by Scotland, Jimmy was a crowd pleaser and delighted supporters throughout his time on Tyneside.

HUGHIE GALLACHER (1925-1930)

'Wee Hughie', as he was affectionately known, was perhaps one of the greatest centre-forwards ever to pull on a Newcastle shirt, and at just 5ft 5", what he lacked in height he made up for in goals – and plenty of them. A tenacious striker, Gallacher's United record is as impressive as any, with the Scot lashing an unbelievable 143 goals in just 174 appearances, including 39 in 41 during the 1926/27 season, where he also skippered the side to League title glory.

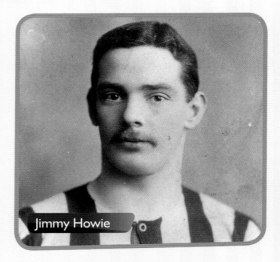

Jimmy Howie

BOBBY MITCHELL (1949-1961)

Along with club colleagues Frank Brennan and Jackie Milburn, Bobby Mitchell was the darling of the Newcastle crowd during the immediate post war years. Known throughout football as 'Bobby Dazzler' he was famed for his immaculate ball control and wing wizardry and scored many an important goal for United, especially in FA Cup ties. A three time Cup winner, Bobby thrilled the United crowd with his magic footwork and ball skills in a 13-year Gallowgate career that saw him hit the net 113 times in 410 appearances. Brought up in the shadows of Hampden Park in Glasgow, Bobby also scored on his debut for Scotland.

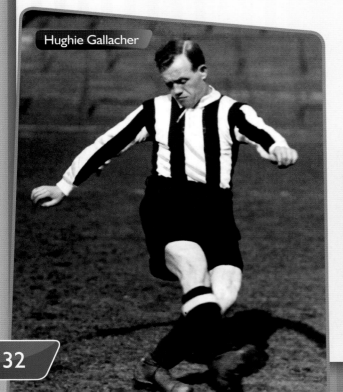

Hughie Gallacher

Bobby Mitchell

Jimmy Smith

PAUL GASCOIGNE (1985-1988)

An FA Youth Cup winner with United in 1985, Gascoigne would go on to become one of the outstanding talents of the game. As a teenager, he possessed an array of skills and flair that rapidly had the whole country taking notice. With superb vision, passing, shooting and dribbling skills to compliment work rate and a huge passion for the game, he was the best of his generation. He did great things with England too, notably in the 1990 World Cup, but after moving to Tottenham and injuring his knee in the 1991 FA Cup Final, he was – sadly – never quite the same player again.

CHRIS WADDLE (1980-1985)

Chris Waddle was an immensely talented ball playing winger who helped set United alight in the early to mid 1980s. Having signed from non league Tow Law, Chris had a slow start at St. James' Park but blossomed into an international class talent, mainly under the astute guidance of manager Arthur Cox. With the rare ability to go past defenders using a body swerve and deceptive pace, Waddle played right across United's front line, putting in dangerous crosses or hitting the target with viciously bending shots. Chris won 62 England caps and played in the 1986 and 1990 World Cups. He is perhaps most 'famous' for missing the vital penalty against West Germany in the semi finals of Italia 90, which eliminated England from the tournament.

JIMMY SMITH (1969-1976)

'Jinky' Jimmy Smith was an outstanding ball player who was United's first 'six-figure' incoming transfer when he moved from Aberdeen. A master craftsman, 'Jinky' could send the crowd into raptures when 'in the mood'. He had a languid, lazy style and possessed a tantalising right foot. Hampered by knee injuries, he was good enough to win international honours for Scotland. His magical performances mean he will always be remembered as one of United's finest.

Paul Gascoigne

Chris Waddle

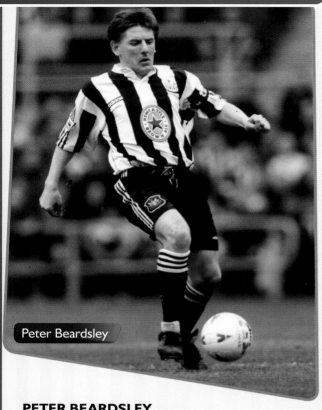

Peter Beardsley

Nobby was a dead-ball expert and first class crosser who created many chances from wide positions. He earned a glittering reputation at an early age in Peru, where he started his career with Alianza Lima before joining Sporting Cristal in 1992. Scorer of over 50 goals in seven seasons in South America, and capped at the early age of 19 for Peru, Nobby went on to play 95 times for his country.

DAVID GINOLA (1995-1997)

An outstanding talent, David joined Kevin Keegan's side from Paris St Germain. A virtuoso of the highest quality, he had immaculate balance and poise, was two-footed and in his first season on Tyneside, delivered the goods with entertainment to boot. Able to bamboozle every defender in the land, Ginola's wing play was exceptional. A pin-up star too, Ginola was a rare talent who thrilled supporters on both sides of the Channel. Sadly he never really made his mark with the French National Team.

PETER BEARDSLEY (1983-1987 & 1993-1997)

A true United legend, Peter appeared for the Magpies in two separate spells, first with the likes of Kevin Keegan and Chris Waddle in the mid 1980s, and then under Keegan the Manager, 10 years on when the Magpies took the Premiership by storm. Peter is recognised by many as the best player to have pulled on the black and white shirt, slight of build but possessing fantastic ball skills and marvellous vision.

The holder of 59 England caps, Peter scored 119 goals in 326 appearances for United, many of which were truly spectacular – the end product of splendid placement, precision timing or delightful dribbles.

NOBBY SOLANO (1998-2004 & 2005-2007)

Nobby became the first Peruvian to play in England when he came to Newcastle via Boca Juniors of Argentina in August 1998. A slight but skilful ball-player,

Nobby Solano

David Ginola

Ayoze

Colback

Ferreyra

De Jong

Riviere

Janmaat

Cabella

1990s

We looked at the 1970s and 1980s in the 2014 annual, so this time we're jumping forward two decades to look at two very exciting periods in United's history.

The 1990s began with bitter disappointment. United, under Jim Smith, were pushing for promotion back to the top flight but had to settle for a Play Off place and a match-up with local rivals Sunderland in the semi-finals. United lost, say no more! The next two seasons in Division Two were no better, and with the club hovering on the brink, Newcastle United needed a saviour. They not only found one, but two, as Sir John Hall and Kevin Keegan joined forces to create a formidable duo. When Keegan returned to Tyneside to replace Ossie Ardiles as manager on a short term contract in 1992, United were struggling at the wrong end of Division Two. Sir John had all but taken control of the club and he needed a small miracle to stop the Magpies from tumbling into the Third Division for the very first time in their history. If Sir John was to transform the near bankrupt club, they simply had to survive relegation.

Just as before, when Keegan was a player ten years earlier, his mere presence captivated the region. United's disgruntled supporters became excited, expectant ones overnight. They packed St James' Park again and United survived. Sir John Hall now turned his attention to a master plan to develop Newcastle United into one of the super clubs of Europe. Kevin Keegan stayed on as manager, and immediately the powerful duo swung into action. The club's finances were transformed and St James' Park redeveloped into a stadium as good as any. Keegan brought in new players, many international superstars. It was the start of a special five years under his guidance.

The First Division Championship was secured in 1993 which included a club record winning run of 11 games at the start of that season. Premier League clubs were faced with a new influence in the game. The Black 'n' Whites joined the elite for the 1993-94 season, and United very quickly became recognised as a force claiming two Runners-Up spots and just missing out on the Title. The club invested heavily in players, and United's squad was a virtual all international one containing players from throughout the globe. Players like David Ginola and Tino Asprilla from abroad, and British stars like Alan Shearer and Duncan Ferguson.

Season 1995/96 was particularly galling for the club. Things were brilliant at times, as United built up what seemed like an unassailable 12-point lead at the top of the table shortly after Christmas, only for Alex Ferguson's men to hunt United down and pip them for the title on the final day of the season – it would have been their first top-flight Championship since 1927!

United though were dubbed the 'Entertainers' for the brand of exciting and attacking football they played. A club with a proud tradition and a fervent and loyal support, United were shocked when Keegan unexpectedly departed in December 1996. However, under the management of Kenny Dalglish, Newcastle entered the Champions League, famously defeating the mighty Barcelona on a heady night on Tyneside. The black 'n' whites reached the FA Cup final in 1998 only to fall to Arsenal. With another world personality in control, Ruud Gullit, Newcastle again reached the FA Cup final only to lose, this time to Manchester United in 1999. After a poor start to the new season, the United board decided it was time for a new direction once again in September 1999, and made what would prove to be an astute appointment – former England manager and local lad Bobby Robson.

CROSSWORD

ACROSS

1 Portuguese defender on loan in 1999/2000. (6)
2 Left back in Entertainers team of 90s. (9)
6 World Cup hosts. (6)
8 Signed from Ajax in 2012. (5)
9 Four-time World Cup winners. (5)
10 Signed from Leeds, sold to Real Madrid. (8)
13 Left back Olivier. (7)
14 Midfielder signed from Ipswich in 2003. (7)
15 The General. (3)

DOWN

1 United's longest serving player. (6)
2 Warren or Joey. (6)
3 On loan French striker in 1999. (4)
4 French winger born in Reunion Islands. (6)
5 Centre half nicknamed 'Killer'. (8)
7 Brazilian defender. (6)
11 Didier. (4)
12 United's Ivorian. (5)

ANSWERS ON PAGE 63

2000s

CHAMPIONS 2010   CHAMPIONS 2010

With Sir Bobby Robson at the helm from 1999-2004, the Magpies developed into a major power in the game, on and off the field. This was demonstrated by consecutive finishing positions of fourth and third in the Premier League in 2001/02 and 2002/03 respectively, and playing in a magnificently redeveloped 52,339 capacity St James' Park. In December 2001, United reached the summit of the Premier League after an outstanding 3-1 midweek win at Highbury. They followed that up with a thrilling 4-3 on-the-road win at Leeds United four days later.

Robson brought in players such as Laurent Robert, Jermaine Jenas and Jonathan Woodgate, and these proved to be masterful signings, adding pace and power to the team. The Magpies also reached the second group phase of the 2002/03 UEFA Champions League. United lost their first three group games but remarkably became the first side to qualify for the second phase after such a poor start. The Magpies won their last three games, including a heart-stopping last minute Craig Bellamy winner in Rotterdam against Feyenoord. Over 10,000 United fans then saw their side draw 2-2 in the San Siro before a last game loss to Barcelona eliminated them from the competition.

The following season, United were devastated to lose on penalties in the Champions League Qualifying Round to Partizan Belgrade, and although they finished fifth in the Premier League, it could have been better.

A bad start to the 2004/05 campaign sadly saw Bobby leave the club with former Liverpool great Graeme Souness appointed in his place. United reached the FA Cup Semi Finals and UEFA Cup Quarter Finals but bowed out of both competitions inside the space of four sorrow-filled days. Souness oversaw the signing of Michael Owen in August 2005 for a club record of £16m, but sadly, injury prevented the England striker from showing his best form on Tyneside. United had slipped to 15th in the first week of February 2006 when the board decided to replace the Scot with 1980s captain Glenn Roeder in a caretaker capacity, later to become permanent in May 2006.

That month also saw the retirement of goal-scoring legend Alan Shearer, who after 206 goals for his beloved home-town club, finally called it a day. After one full season in charge, Glenn Roeder resigned and Sam Allardyce, who left Bolton in April 2007, took over only to leave in January 2008. United needed some stability, and in mid January, under the ownership of Mike Ashley, Kevin Keegan returned to the Club as Manager. However, he was only back at St. James' Park for eight months until his resignation in September 2008.

After the brief stewardship of Joe Kinnear and Alan Shearer in 2008/09, a season that ultimately ended in grave disappointment on the field with relegation, Chris Hughton was appointed Manager in October 2009 and led the team to the Coca-Cola Championship title in record breaking style, earning a magnificent 102 points. 'Captain Kevin Nolan led a team of stalwarts such as Steve Harper, Alan Smith, Nicky Butt and Joey Barton with rising stars like Andy Carroll, giving the supporters pride in their side once more. An amazing average of over 43,000 fans cheered them on at St. James' Park every other week.

WORDSEARCH

See if you can find 20 players who played Premier League football for Newcastle in the 2000s.

T	E	V	L	R	E	K	R	A	P	L	M	B	P
H	T	T	B	U	P	D	P	E	X	R	I	E	Z
B	A	C	R	K	Q	K	L	S	M	M	L	L	C
M	G	N	P	E	H	U	B	O	E	O	N	L	J
T	D	T	T	U	B	R	E	R	R	W	E	A	N
A	O	R	Y	J	A	O	E	B	T	E	R	M	A
K	O	R	A	M	Z	G	R	M	K	N	G	Y	L
U	W	N	B	G	B	A	B	A	Y	A	R	O	I
D	R	L	R	R	D	H	K	A	T	D	O	R	V
I	E	N	R	S	T	E	A	B	S	N	L	R	A
V	R	N	A	Y	K	N	T	T	Y	S	T	N	G
M	L	N	L	N	U	G	H	E	Z	H	O	T	P
T	E	M	M	C	Q	G	W	Z	N	F	M	N	T
J	Q	N	A	K	L	U	I	V	E	R	T	N	G

Acuna	Bramble	Jenas	Owen
Ambrose	Butt	Kluivert	Parker
Babayaro	Edgar	Luque	Robert
Bassong	Gavilan	Milner	Viduka
Bellamy	Geremi	Onyewu	Woodgate

ANSWERS ON PAGE 63

GOING UP WITH
THE MAGPIES

Nearly every stadium up and down the country offers stadium tours which include areas such as the changing rooms, media suite and pitchside access, but in 2014, Newcastle United launched something completely different to supplement the usual tour…

The new exciting, even hair-raising, Newcastle United Roof Top Stadium Tours are something no supporter will want to miss. The incredible views inside and around St. James' Park all add up to an awesome, spine-tingling and exhilarating journey.

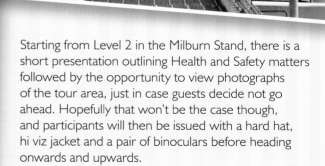

Starting from Level 2 in the Milburn Stand, there is a short presentation outlining Health and Safety matters followed by the opportunity to view photographs of the tour area, just in case guests decide not go ahead. Hopefully that won't be the case though, and participants will then be issued with a hard hat, hi viz jacket and a pair of binoculars before heading onwards and upwards.

During the tour there will always be two guides, one at the front and one at the back. Once on the roof, there will be view point arrows showing the route across the roof, and in addition, there are three viewing platforms where visitors can read about the landmarks they can see.

Those on the tour will get unprecedented access and magnificent views of the city and beyond in what in many ways is a sightseeing tour rather than a St James' Park stadium tour, although you do get a superb, if not distant, view of the pitch. At the conclusion of the tour, guests will be taken down pitch side to take in the majestic internal view of the stadium and look up in awe at where they've just been.

"From virtually the highest point in the city, you can see for miles and miles in all directions and it all adds up to quite a unique and sensational experience."

20 YEARS IN TOON

When Steve Harper finished his career at Newcastle United at the end of the 2012/13 season, he left with the record of being United's longest serving player, a 20-year stint on Tyneside. Fittingly, he was rewarded with a 'testimonial' in September 2013, which effectively was a charity match generously benefitting six North East Charities and raising a staggering £328,000.

The match was against an AC Milan XI and involved many United heroes from the past 20 years including the likes of Alan Shearer, Peter Beardsley, David Ginola and Les Ferdinand.

These pictures illustrate what a fantastic and emotion filled-evening it was at St. James' Park in front of an incredible 50,793 fans.

Steve was signed for United from non-league football in 1993, but took six years to break into the first team and then played in the 1999 FA Cup Final against Manchester United in his 10th senior match.

"Over 50,000 fans came to see the United and Milan legends."

Steve saved the penalty at Watford on 7 November 2006, which earned United their first competitive penalty shoot-out success – after seven consecutive losses.

From the start of the 2009/10 season, Harper, after conceding at West Brom on the opening day of the season, went 501 minutes before picking the ball out of the back of the net again, at Blackpool, on 16 September 2009.

Steve had already made sure he would be in United's record books by keeping the most clean sheets in a season for the club, passing Willie McFaul's previous individual best and setting the best overall in any United season, 21 (the team record was 22) in 2009/10.

At the end of the 2009/10 season he created a notable achievement of being involved in over 550 senior matches – either on the pitch or on the bench. No other United player had reached that total.

In the 2012/13 season, Steve became the club's longest serving player in nearly 130 years since the club was formed in 1881. Harper first pulled on the United 'keeper's jersey as a youngster back in December 1991 in a Northern Intermediate League game against Middlesbrough. The previous record service as a player of nearly 19 years by stalwarts of pre-war days, Bill McCracken and Frank Hudspeth, was passed by Steve, with it being his 20th as a United player.

> **Steve was awarded the Wilkinson Sword by Sport Newcastle on 12 March 2012 for services to sport and the community.**

Last season, Steve joined Hull City and helped the Tigers to Wembley for the FA Cup Final, playing his part in the semi-final win over Sheffield United on the hallowed Wembley turf.

PLAYER QUIZ

Can you match the Nationality of these 20 past and present United players?

Jon-Dahl Tomasson

Uruguay

Mark Viduka

Croatia

Christian Bassedas

Argentina

Haris Vuckic

Slovenia

Spain

David Rozehnal

Portugal

George Georgiadis

Finland

Cyprus

Silvio Maric

Shefki Kuqi

Celestine Babayaro

Scotland

Rep of Ireland

Canada

Ignacio Gonzalez

David Edgar

Greece

Hugo Viana

Nigeria

Niki Papavasiliou

Denmark

Australia

France

John Karelse

Abdoulaye Faye

Alain Goma

Giuseppe Rossi

Albert Luque

Italy

Senegal

Damien Duff

Czech Republic

Holland

Stephen Glass

ANSWERS ON PAGE 62

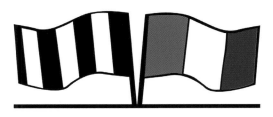

THE FRENCH CONNECTION

By the end of the 2013/14 season, 185 players had represented United in the Premier League. Naturally the majority of these (73) were English, but the country with the next highest contingent of players is France with 24. Here we plot them all from their place of birth together with the number of games played and goals scored in all competitions.

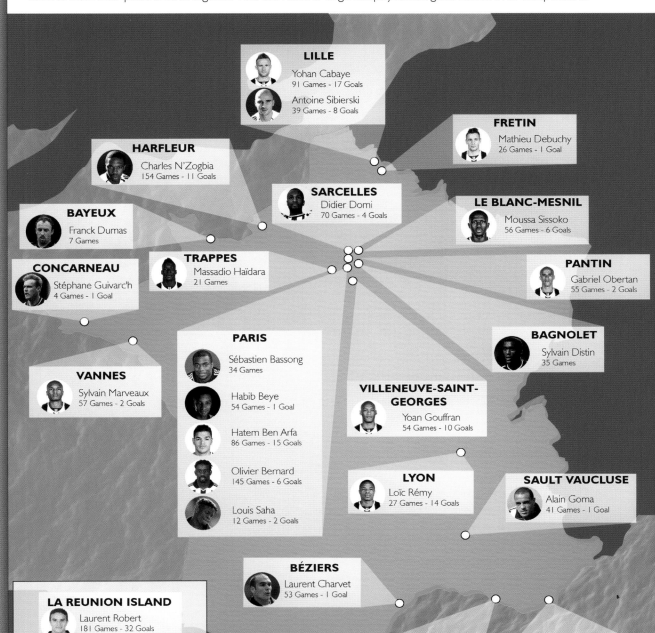

LILLE
Yohan Cabaye
91 Games - 17 Goals
Antoine Sibierski
39 Games - 8 Goals

FRETIN
Mathieu Debuchy
26 Games - 1 Goal

HARFLEUR
Charles N'Zogbia
154 Games - 11 Goals

SARCELLES
Didier Domi
70 Games - 4 Goals

LE BLANC-MESNIL
Moussa Sissoko
56 Games - 6 Goals

BAYEUX
Franck Dumas
7 Games

TRAPPES
Massadio Haïdara
21 Games

PANTIN
Gabriel Obertan
55 Games - 2 Goals

CONCARNEAU
Stéphane Guivarc'h
4 Games - 1 Goal

BAGNOLET
Sylvain Distin
35 Games

PARIS
Sébastien Bassong
34 Games

Habib Beye
54 Games - 1 Goal

Hatem Ben Arfa
86 Games - 15 Goals

Olivier Bernard
145 Games - 6 Goals

Louis Saha
12 Games - 2 Goals

VANNES
Sylvain Marveaux
57 Games - 2 Goals

VILLENEUVE-SAINT-GEORGES
Yoan Gouffran
54 Games - 10 Goals

LYON
Loïc Rémy
27 Games - 14 Goals

SAULT VAUCLUSE
Alain Goma
41 Games - 1 Goal

BÉZIERS
Laurent Charvet
53 Games - 1 Goal

LA REUNION ISLAND
Laurent Robert
181 Games - 32 Goals

GASSIN
David Ginola
75 Games - 7 Goals

PORT-DE-BOUC
Mapou Yanga-Mbiwa*
46 Games

**Mapou Yanga-Mbiwa was atually born in Bangui, Central African Republic, however was raised in Port-de-Bouc and plays for the French national team.*

45

UNITED IN THE COMMUNITY

...olo Supports Toon Times

Toon Times is an educational programme which uses the power of football to improve the literacy and learning techniques of young people. The project will reach 15,000 youngsters across 430 Tyneside schools over three years, with historic Magpies artefacts and props helping to bring the past to life. Fabricio Coloccini joined in a football coaching session and looked back at some of United's iconic football shirts with the children.

Rob Gets His Kicks

Rob Elliot was at Redheugh FC to launch the Kicks project for Newcastle United Foundation. Kicks is a Premier League initiative which aims to build safer, stronger communities and help young people achieve goals through football. One of the main objectives of Kicks is to encourage volunteering and create routes into education, training and employment. Another key objective is to reduce crime and anti-social behaviour in the neighbourhood.

Santon Helps the Youngsters

Davide Santon cast an eye over Tyneside's young footballing talent as part of the Newcastle United Foundation's Holiday Soccer Schools. Santon joined in with their coaching session; which included fun games, skill challenges and small-sided matches as well as a focus on the importance of respect, fair play, anti-bullying and discipline across all levels of the game.

Hospital Cheer

The full first team squad visit the region's local hospitals just before Christmas each year and it's always a fun-filled time for the players and children. Here Papiss Cisse, Vurnon Anita and Cheick Tiote are delivering Christmas cheer to one of the Royal Victoria Infirmary's young patients. The players give presents to all the children as well as donating money to the Children's Unit at the Hospital.

Local Lads at the Museum

Newcastle United players attended the launch of Toon Times exhibition, held at the Discovery Museum, which takes supporters on a journey through the Club's history. Shola Ameobi, Sammy Ameobi and Paul Dummett were joined by Fairs Cup-winning captain Bob Moncur, Steve Harper, Olivier Bernard and Brian Kilcline for a special preview of historic artefacts and interactive displays.

Howay the Lasses

Wonga.com, the digital finance company, which became the first organisation to sponsor both the men's and women's clubs in 2014, arranged for Combative Ivory Coast midfielder Cheick Tiote to drop in to a training session at Northumbria University's Coach Lane campus, where the ladies were being put through their paces by first team coach, Trevor Benjamin. 'Howay the Lasses' was the message happily delivered by Cheick!

Reading Star Sammy

Sammy Ameobi, Newcastle United's Premier League Reading Star, teamed up with the National Literary Trust to promote the benefits of reading to Tyneside schoolchildren. Ameobi said: "I've always been a huge fan of reading. It has a really positive impact on my life and helps me to relax away from football, so it's great to be involved with Premier League Reading Stars and to be teaching local school kids about how reading can really help them."

Willo Supports School Sport

Mike Williamson visited Walkergate Primary School to help the Foundation launch a brand new schools football coaching initiative. The Premier League School Sports Project saw the Magpies' charity offer a package to 48 primary schools in 2014; including in-school coaching, after-school clubs, competitions and teacher training. The aim is to encourage both girls and boys to take part in regular sport and physical activity

Good Tasting Pizzas

Newcastle United signed up with the Papa John's pizza company in 2014 and it was a partnership that provided plenty of good tasting pizzas for the fans. There were a number of competitions run by the club with Papa John's where fans could get pizzas at half price, and some supporters even had their pizzas personally delivered by the United players!

MATHS
CHALLENGE

A quiz with a difference! This not only teaches you about Newcastle United but lets you get to grips with some tricky maths challenges. Work out the questions below – the answer is the number of a current squad player.

3

Clean Sheets in the 2013/14 Premier League season

✕

The round number that Newcastle reached in the 2013/14 League Cup

÷

Gael Bigirimana's squad number

=

1

The year the club was formed

÷

Adam Armstrong's squad number in 2013/14

=

Tim Krul's 2013/14 Premier League appearances

=

4

The year St. James' Park was increased to a 52,000 capacity

–

The year Kevin Keegan joined Newcastle United for the first time

÷

The total number of times Newcastle have won the FA Cup

=

2

Davide Santon's squad number

+

Newcastle's points in the 2013/14 Premier League season

–

Newcastle's goals scored in the 2013/14 Premier League season

=

5

The total number of games Newcastle United played in the Inter Cities Fairs Cup in 1969

+

Total number of goals Alan Shearer scored for England

÷

The number of times United have lost in the FA Cup Final

=

ANSWERS ON PAGE 62

GOALS 2013/14

It wasn't a vintage season for goals, but that doesn't mean the ten we have selected here aren't up with the best we've seen in recent years, both at St. James' Park and on the road. As ever, there were plenty of crackers to choose from with departed French pair Yohan Cabaye and Loic Remy to the fore.

HATEM BEN ARFA
V FULHAM H, 31/8/13

The first goal of the season at St. James' Park and with only four minutes remaining. Hatem Ben Arfa's touch, control, trickery and fleet of foot were all evident in the build up to his match-winning effort. Chesting down a crossfield ball, the mercurial wideman bamboozled the Cottagers' defence before cutting inside past John Arne Riise and Alex Kacaniklic to curl a left-foot strike past a helpless David Stockdale, sending the Gallowgate End wild – a real classy goal.

YOAN GOUFFRAN
V LEEDS UNITED H, 25/9/13

United were one up in this League Cup tie when on 67 minutes, Sammy Ameobi once again created the opportunity. Taking a pass on the left flank, he jinked infield before nudging the ball forward to Yoan Gouffran just inside the box. The former Bordeaux man had his back to the goal, but took a touch to turn away from marker Scott Wootton to deliver a ferocious right foot finish, notching his first goal at St. James' Park.

YOHAN CABAYE
V EVERTON A, 30/9/13

It had been a nightmare first 45 minutes for United, 3-0 down to the Toffees and the home side rampant. But shortly after the restart the fightback began. Yoan Gouffran moved the ball in from the United left before laying off a short ball to Yohan Cabaye, who, without ceremony, skillfully struck it with his right foot into the top right hand corner of Tim Howard's goal from outside the Everton box, dipping just as it crossed the line – unstoppable.

LOIC REMY
V CARDIFF A, 5/10/13

After back-to-back defeats, a good result at the Cardiff City stadium was imperative as United looked to get their league campaign back on track. On the half hour, Loic Remy danced his way forward from the halfway line and cut inside two defenders before hitting the ball low and hard inside David Marshall's post from the edge of the box. It was a goal typical of the on-loan Frenchman and his fourth in three games.

LOIC REMY
V CHELSEA H, 2/11/13

Not necessarily the most stunning goal you will see, but beautiful in its own way in terms of seeing off the Londoners. With the 90 minutes almost up, Remy's initial shot was blocked, and when the ball ended up towards the left touchline in the possession of Gabriel Obertan and Vurnon Anita, the two substitutes combined nicely before the latter negotiated two challenges before pulling the ball back for Remy to drill home a left-footed shot via the left hand post. St. James' Park erupted.

GOALS 2013/14

MOUSSA SISSOKO
V WEST BROM H, 30/11/13

Moussa Sissoko's rocket against West Brom was a real thunderbolt struck with awesome power and accuracy. With United searching for a winner, a triangle of passes on halfway between Cabaye and Gouffran led to Davide Santon flicking the ball forward. Controlled headers from Ameobi and Remy saw it arrive with Sissoko, who took a touch before crashing home an unstoppable right foot strike past Boaz Myhill from 25 yards. Pick that one out!

YOHAN CABAYE
V STOKE CITY H, 26/12/13

Another Yohan Cabaye classic. With United strolling to victory against nine-man Stoke, Massadio Haidara checked his left wing run and slipped a pass back to Sissoko, who picked out Debuchy on the opposite side of the area. His header across the box was nodded down by Ameobi to Gouffran, who swapped passes with Debuchy before Cabaye arrived to side-foot in beautifully. Undoubtedly the team goal of the season.

LOIC REMY
V ASTON VILLA H, 23/2/14

Into injury time and United were searching for a dramatic winner. Luuk De Jong tried a snapshot on the right edge of the box that was blocked and the ball looped up and landed at Remy's feet. He still had to control it and side-step Vlaar before thumping the ball left-footed past Brad Guzan. Off came the shirt as Loic headed into the crowd in the Gallowgate corner with his teammates ecstatically mobbing him.

MOUSSA SISSOKO
V HULL CITY A, 1/3/14

Simple and straightforward but a really wonderful strike. After only 10 minutes, in what would turn out to be United's best away win of the season, Tim Krul's lengthy throw to Moussa Sissoko on the left initiated a quick counter-attack and as the ball was fed between Yoan Gouffran, Cheick Tiote and Loic Remy. Sissoko strode upfield to crash the ball home from 12 yards when Mathieu Debuchy delivered from the right flank. Take that!

YOHAN CABAYE
V MANCHESTER UNITED
A, 7/12/13

A superb, disciplined and clinical team performance brought United the three points for the first time since 1972. Tim Krul's long clearance fell to Moussa Sissoko out on the right and he strode forward before pulling the ball back for Yohan Cabaye to side-foot past David De Gea from the edge of the box. Pursued by his colleagues, Cabaye went to ground by the corner flag in front of the joyous away fans and was then the unfortunate recipient of what can only be described as a mass pile-on.

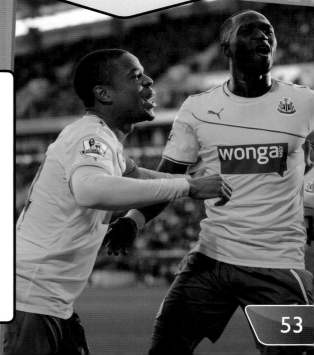

TO THE GLORY OF GOD, FOR RIGHT, LIBERTY & PEACE

The national commemoration of the 100th anniversary of the start of World War One kicked in at the start of the 2014/15 season, and like all football clubs, Newcastle United marked the centenary, focussing on the many players and officials who served in the Great War, with some sadly never to return.

BRITISH INFANTRYMEN marching towards the front lines in the River Somme valley.

War was declared on 4 August 1914, and although football continued for that 1914-15 season, as battles developed and intensified as well as worsened, it was clear that the sport could not keep going as normal.

To start with, fixtures at St James' Park saw many fans dressed in forces uniform as the call to arms gathered pace. Gradually, injured soldiers were to be seen in the crowd too. Then players began joining local regiments, and firing practice was carried out by United's footballers on the Gallowgate pitch – with rifles rather than footballs. War put a stop to football at the end of the season.

Situated within the Milburn Stand covered walkway, next to the Atrium entrance, is an engraved plaque to all those players and officials on the club's staff to have served in the military. The plaque is titled 'To The Glory of God'…. they….'Fought for Right, Liberty & Peace' and was erected in 1919, shortly after peace was restored. This historic memorial was recently restored and brought to life when a Museum was opened at Gallowgate at the start of the Nineties.

Thousands upon thousands of United fans pass the Roll of Honour every match day and can see what is a very poignant memorial, especially in this special year of remembrance. In all, thirteen past or present Newcastle footballers were killed on the Continent. Their names should be remembered:

DAN DUNGLINSON
TOM CAIRNS
RICHARD MCGOUGH
TOMMY GOODWILL
GEORGE RIVERS
DONALD BELL
JOHN FINDLAY
JOHN FLEMING
TOM HUGHES
JAMES MAXWELL
TOM ROWLANDSON
CHARLES RANDALL
NICHOLAS HIGGINS

NEWCASTLE UNITED'S FIRST WORLD WAR MEMORIAL
situated in the Milburn Stand walkway.

There are many other ex-players who fought on the Continent not listed on the club's memorial, including one of the very few footballer VC winners, Donald Simpson Bell, a reserve player at the club in 1911-12. The club are very proud that a former player was honoured with the highest honour, although tragically, Bell was killed shortly after his heroic deed in 1916 with the Green Howards.

Several other players were honoured. Scottish international Sandy Higgins earned the Military Medal as did Finlay Speedie, a teammate in Newcastle's celebrated line-up, and also another capped player for the Scots. Higgins, a top-class forward for United during the Edwardian heyday, served with the Durham Light Infantry and Yorkshire Regiment.

Many life or death stories are related involving United's footballers. Tommy Goodwill and Dan Dunglinson joined up together in the Northumberland Fusiliers and died together as they climbed from the trenches in the opening battle of the Somme. Their names are included at the huge and poignant Thiepval Memorial in France. So many others are also to be found on memorials throughout the battlefields of France and Belgium.

Past goalkeeper Tom Rowlandson was another to be on the Somme fields. An amateur and famous Corinthian footballer, he was at Gallowgate in 1905-06 and enlisted with the Yorkshire regiment. Tom won the Military Cross for gallant exploits during the Somme offensive, but was killed leading his men from the front. Harry Thompson was a reserve left-back with United and also joined the local DLI, but was badly wounded with leg injuries. He could not resurrect a footballing career once peace was established.

Newcastle players also joined the celebrated Footballer's Battalion of the Middlesex Regiment; Jack Doran, George Pyke and John Dodds included. Jimmy Low, with Hearts at the beginning of the conflict, was one of several players from Tynecastle to join up en-masse, into McCrae's Battalion of Royal Scots. Low survived, although he was twice wounded, and went onto play for United during the Twenties. He lifted the FA Cup with United at Wembley in 1924.

TOMMY GOODWILL, along with Dan Dunglinson, a reserve amateur centre-forward with the club, was killed at the Somme battlefield.

CATERPILLAR VALLEY CEMETERY on the Somme, France. The bodies of 150,000 Commonwealth servicemen lie buried across the scarred rural landscape that forms the Somme battlefields.

SPOT THE DIFFERENCE

Can you spot the 10 differences in this picture of Liverpool v Newcastle, May 2014?

ANSWERS ON PAGE 63

GOALSCORING FILE

Shola Ameobi signed off his United career in May 2014, scoring in his last two games at St. James' Park and finishing with 79 NUFC career goals. The big man then hit a career highlight by proudly representing Nigeria in the 2014 World Cup in Brazil.

Shola was a hugely talented striker with a penchant for the unpredictable, who made his first team debut against Chelsea in September 2000 – and memorably squared up to Dennis Wise to show his intent that he wasn't to be messed with. Born in Nigeria, Shola came to England with his parents at the age of five and attended the Newcastle United Academy from the age of 13 as well as representing Walker Central Boys Club. Tall and deceptively languid, Shola had great skill on the ground and his exciting form with the Academy earned him a Reserve team debut the day before his 18th birthday. He then went on to make his debut for the England U21 side in 2000/01.

Shola showed his class with a well taken goal and terrific all round display against Barcelona in the Champions League in the Nou Camp and followed that up with a superb double in Leverkusen, helping

him towards 15 European goals for the club, second only to Alan Shearer. Shola netted his first senior United hat-trick against Reading at St. James' Park in August 2009 and was named Coca-Cola Championship Player of the Month in August 2009. Two goals against Sunderland in October 2010 took him into second place (behind Jackie Milburn) in the goal scoring charts for goals scored (7) against United's fiercest rivals. He started with brother Sammy against Brugge in November 2011, the first brothers to start a United game together in a competitive environment since the Robledo brothers in the 1950s. Shola earned his first full international cap (Nigeria) against Venezuela in November 2012 in Miami, and scored his first international goal in Nigeria's 4–1 win over Burkina Faso in September 2013.

Here we look at Shola's goalscoring career at the club, with the infographic opposite displaying his career in graphic style.

	League	FA Cup	Lge Cup	Europe	Total
2000/01	12 (8) 2	2 (0) 0	0 (0) 0	0 (0) 0	14 (8) 2
2001/02	4 (11) 0	0 (1) 0	2 (1) 2	6 (0) 3	12 (13) 5
2002/03	8 (20) 5	0 (1) 0	0 (0) 0	4 (6) 3	12 (27) 8
2003/04	18 (8) 7	0 (1) 0	1 (0) 0	8 (5) 3	27 (14) 10
2004/05	17 (14) 2	3 (2) 3	1 (1) 1	6 (1) 1	27 (18) 7
2005/06	25 (5) 9	3 (0) 0	0 (0) 0	0 (1) 0	28 (6) 9
2006/07	9 (3) 3	0 (0) 0	0 (0) 0	2 (2) 2	11 (5) 5
2007/08	2 (4) 0	0 (0) 0	2 (0) 0	0 (0) 0	4 (4) 0
2008/09	14 (8) 4	0 (0) 0	0 (0) 0	0 (0) 0	14 (8) 4
2009/10	11 (7) 10	1 (1) 0	0 (1) 1	0 (0) 0	12 (9) 11
2010/11	21 (7) 6	0 (0) 0	2 (0) 3	0 (0) 0	23 (7) 9
2011/12	8 (19) 2	1 (1) 0	0 (1) 0	0 (0) 0	9 (21) 2
2012/13	4 (19) 1	1 (0) 0	1 (0) 0	5 (5) 3	11 (24) 4
2013/14	14 (12) 2	0 (1) 0	1 (1) 1	0 (0) 0	15 (14) 3
Total	**167 (145) 53**	**11 (8) 3**	**10 (5) 8**	**31 (20) 15**	**219 (178) 79**

23

SHOLA AMEOBI
Newcastle United September 2000–May 2014

STARTS	APPEARANCES	SUBSTITUTE APPEARANCES
219	397	178

HEADERS **16**

WHERE SCORED

HOME **46** — Scored in **69** games — AWAY **33**

SCORED AGAINST

Sunderland
Middlesbrough
Birmingham, Bolton, Chelsea, Coventry, Reading, Wigan
Fulham, Ipswich, Leverkusen, Liverpool, Lillestrom, Lokeren, Manchester City, Manchester United, Sheffield Wednesday, Southampton, Tottenham Hotspur, Valerenga, West Bromwich Albion
Accrington Stanley, Aston Villa, Barcelona, Basel, Bordeaux, Brentford, Club Brugge, Cardiff, Everton, Huddersfield, Leeds, Leicester, Metalist Kharkiv, Morecambe, Norwich, Nottingham Forest, Peterborough, Portsmouth, QPR, Sochaux, Swansea, Troyes, Wolves, Yeading

GOAL KEY
1 Hat-trick
8 Braces
60 Single Strikes

SCORED AND UNITED **WON** **48 70%** **DREW** **12 17%** **LOST** **9 13%**

PENALTIES

10/10   **100%**

COMPETITION GOALS

PREMIER LEAGUE **43**
CHAMPIONSHIP **10**
FA CUP **3**
LEAGUE CUP **8**
CHAMPIONS LEAGUE **3**
EUROPA LEAGUE **7**
INTERTOTO CUP **5**

RIGHT FOOT **47**
LEFT FOOT **16**

GOALS

	1	2	3	4	5	6	7	8	9	10	11	MANAGERS SCORED FOR ⬇
2000/01												
2001/02												SIR BOBBY ROBSON **25**
2002/03												
2003/04												
2004/05												GRAEME SOUNESS **9**
2005/06												
2006/07												GLENN ROEDER **12**
2007/08 (ON LOAN)												
2008/09												JOE KINNEAR **4**
2009/10												CHRIS HUGHTON **14**
2010/11												
2011/12												ALAN PARDEW **12**
2012/13												
2013/14												

TOTAL GOALS **79**

TIME SCORED

1-15 mins	16-30 mins	31-45 mins	46-60 mins	61-75 mins	76-90 mins
6	17	18	11	16	11

GOAL CELEBRATIONS

There have been many varied and enjoyable goal celebrations seen over the years at St. James' Park. Here are a selection of some of the most recent and distinctive ones which we're sure you'll remember only too well, ranging from Oba Martins' somersault to the trademark 'arm in the air' from Alan Shearer.

Demba Ba

Oba Martins

Kevin Nolan

Andy Carroll

Shola Ameobi

Alan Shearer

QUIZ ANSWERS

Three of a Kind Page 20

1. Davide Santon, Giuseppe Rossi, Alessandro Pistone
2. Alan Shearer, Jackie Milburn, Len White
3. Alan Shearer, Les Ferdinand, Andy Cole
4. Jimmy Lawrence, Frank Hudspeth, Alf McMichael
5. Charlie Mitten, Norman Smith, Joe Harvey
6. Everton, Wimbledon, Aston Villa
7. Shearer, Milburn and McMichael
8. Cole, Rossi and Mitten

NUFC Quiz Page 21

What do you remember about the 2013/14 season?

1. Papiss Cisse
2. Cardiff City
3. Everton and Manchester City
4. Five
5. Mathieu Debuchy
6. 1971/72
7. Marseille
8. Arsenal and Manchester City
9. Curtis Good
10. Yohan Cabaye, Loic Remy and Moussa Sissoko

See how much you know about Newcastle United Past and Present!

1. 1972
2. Kevin Keegan
3. Blackburn Rovers
4. Second, Wembley opened in 1923.
5. Aston Villa
6. Grimsby Town
7. Burnley
8. Lazio
9. Swindon and Tottenham
10. Ronny Johnsen

French Quiz Page 23

1. b – Les crampons (Boots)
2. b – Le poteau de but (Goalpost)
3. a – Un journal (Newspaper)
4. d – Le maillot des Bleus (France team shirt)
5. a – Carton jaune (Yellow card)

Player Quiz Page 44

Jon-Dahl Tomasson	Denmark
Mark Viduka	Australia
Christian Bassedas	Argentina
David Rozehnal	Czech Republic
Ignacio Gonzalez	Uruguay
Haris Vuckic	Slovenia
Shefki Kuqi	Finland
Niki Papavasiliou	Cyprus
Silvio Maric	Croatia
David Edgar	Canada
George Georgiadis	Greece
Damien Duff	Rep of Ireland
Celestine Babayaro	Nigeria
Hugo Viana	Portugal
Giuseppe Rossi	Italy
John Karelse	Holland
Albert Luque	Spain
Abdoulaye Faye	Senegal
Alain Goma	France
Stephen Glass	Scotland

Maths Challenge Page 49

1) $1892 \div 43 - 36 =$ Vurnon Anita (8)
2) $3 + 49 - 43 =$ Papiss Cisse (9)
3) $10 \times 4 \div 20 =$ Fabricio Coloccini (2)
4) $2000 - 1982 \div 6 =$ Davide Santon (3)
5) $12 + 30 \div 7 =$ Mike Williamson (6)